t needs ap

buy 2 dozen

e dollar bill.

the cost of a

Madeline's a

pies. Madeline

the grocer

28 cents. What

The Bracelet

Adapted from a story by
Elizabeth Ballard

Illustrated by Miriam de Rosier

Gibbs Smith, Publisher

"The Special Story of Miss Thompson," is found in *Who Switched the Price Tags?* (pp. 69–72), by Tony Campolo. Dallas, Texas, et al: Word Publishing, 1986. Used with permission.

First Edition
07 06 05   7 6 5 4

Text © 2003 by Elizabeth Ballard
Illustrations © 2003 by Miriam de Rosier

Published by
Gibbs Smith, Publisher
P.O. Box 667
Layton, Utah 84041

Orders: (1–800) 748–5439
www.gibbs-smith.com

Edited by Jennifer Adams
Designed by Dawn DeVries Sokol
Printed and bound in China

Library of Congress Cataloging-in-Publication Data

Ballard, Elizabeth.
    The bracelet / by Elizabeth Ballard ; illustrations by Miriam de Rosier.—1st ed.
        p. cm.
      ISBN 1-58685-050-4
      1. Teacher-student relationships—Fiction. 2. Elementary school teachers—
    Fiction. 3. Mothers—Death—Fiction. 4. Women teachers—Fiction. 5. Gifts—
    Fiction. I. Title.

PS3552.A4647 B72 2001
813'.6—dc21

                                                    00-045624

On the first day of school, Jean Thompson told her students, "Boys and girls, I love you all the same. I have no favorites."

Of course, she wasn't being completely truthful. Teachers do have favorites and, what is worse, most teachers have students that they just don't like.

Teddy Stallard was a boy that Miss Thompson just didn't like. He didn't seem interested in school. There was a deadpan, blank expression on his face and his eyes had a glassy, unfocused appearance. When she spoke to Teddy, he always answered in monosyllables. His clothes were musty and his hair was unkempt. He wasn't an attractive boy and he certainly wasn't likable.

Teachers have records. And Jean Thompson had Teddy's.

"First grade: Teddy shows promise with his work and attitude, but poor home situation."

"Second grade: Teddy could do better. Mother is seriously ill. He receives little help at home."

"Third grade: Teddy is a good boy,
but too serious. He is a slow learner. His
mother died this year."

"Fourth grade: Teddy is very slow, but well behaved. His father shows no interest."

Christmas came, and the boys and girls brought their presents and piled them on Miss Thompson's desk. They were all in brightly colored paper except for Teddy's. His was wrapped in brown paper, held together with Scotch tape. On the paper he had written the simple words, "For Miss Thompson from Teddy."

$1.05. His father's gift costs $1.3
others gift co
on sale
$1.50. How
does Pau
For Miss Thompson from Teddy

When she opened Teddy's present, out fell a gaudy rhinestone bracelet, with half the stones missing, and a bottle of cheap perfume.

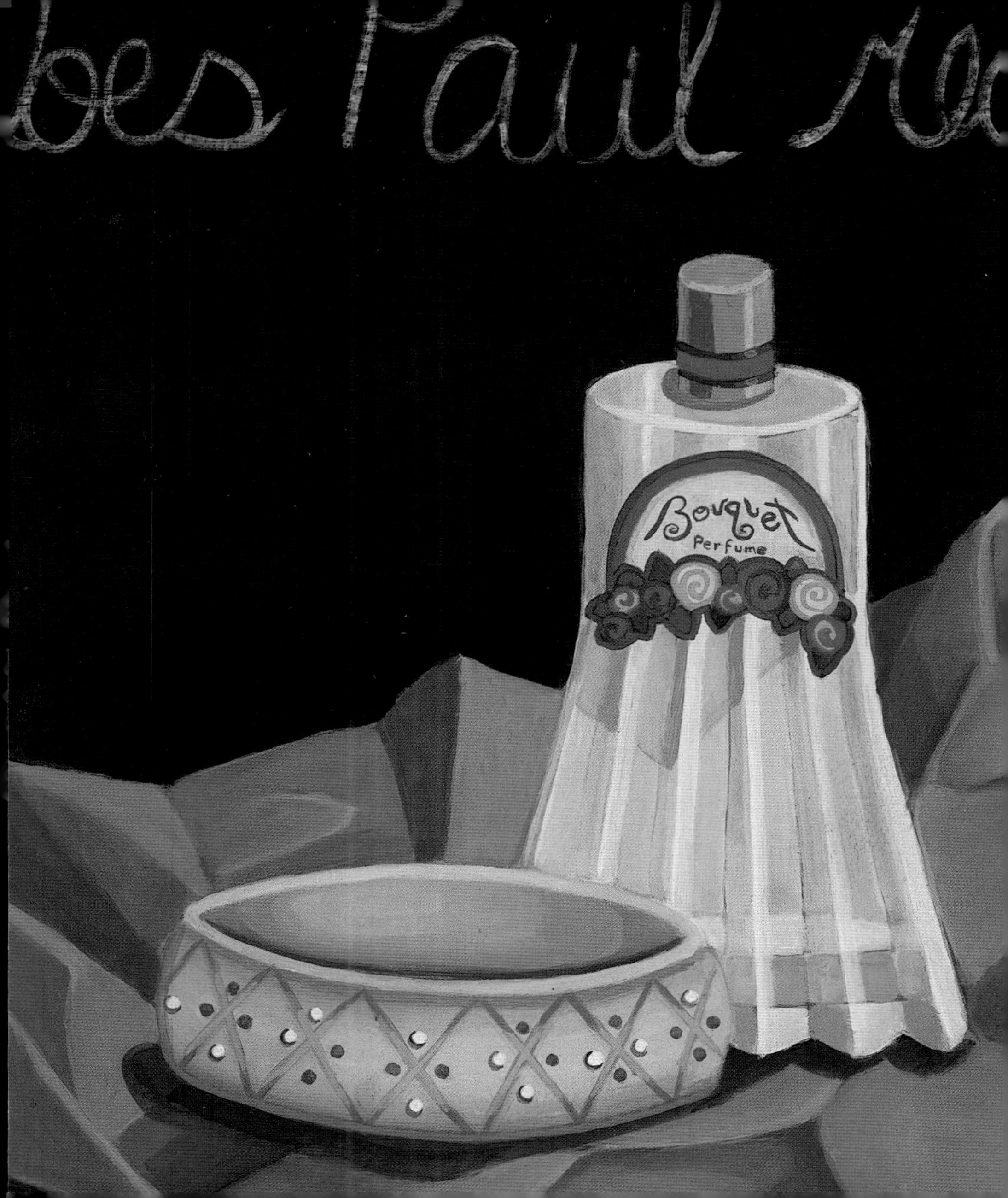
Bouquet
Perfume

Madeline's aunt needs apples to make pies. Madeline buys 2 dozen apples and gives the grocer one dollar bill. Her change is 28 cents. What is the cost of an average apple?

Paul walks into [a] store with $4.00 to buy three [birthday] gifts for his mother, father, and [bro]ther. His mother's gift costs $1.05. H[is father's] gift cost[s] $1.37. H[is] brother's gift [is on] sale for $1.50. H[ow much change does] Paul recei[ve]

When the other boys and girls began to giggle, Miss Thompson had enough sense to silence them by immediately putting on the bracelet and putting some of the perfume on her wrist. Holding her wrist up for the other children to smell, she said, "Doesn't it smell lovely? Isn't the bracelet pretty?" And the children, taking their cue from the teacher, readily agreed.

$\mathcal{A}$t the end of the day, when all the children had left, Teddy lingered, came over to her desk and said, "Miss Thompson, you smell just like my mother. And her bracelet looks real pretty on you too. I'm glad you liked my presents."

When Teddy left, Miss Thompson got down on her knees and asked God to forgive her.

The next day when the children came, Jean Thompson was a different teacher. She helped all the children, but especially the slow ones, and especially Teddy Stallard.

By the end of that school year, Teddy showed dramatic improvement. He had caught up with most of the students and was even ahead of some.

She didn't hear from Teddy for a long time. Then one day, she received a note that read:

Dear Miss Thompson:
  I wanted you to be the first to know.
I will be graduating second in my high school class.

Love,
Teddy Stallard

Four years later, another note came:

Dear Miss Thompson:
  They just told me I will be graduating first in my class. I wanted you to be the first to know. The university has not been easy, but I liked it.

Love,
Teddy Stallard

*A*nd, four years later:

Dear Miss Thompson:

  As of today, I am Theodore J. Stallard,
M.D. How about that? I wanted you
to be the first to know. I am getting
married next month, the 27th to be
exact. I want you to come and sit where
my mother would sit if she were alive.
You are the only family I have now;
Dad died last year.

Love,
Teddy Stallard

$\mathcal{M}$iss Thompson went to that
wedding and sat where Teddy's
mother would have sat. She deserved to
sit there; she had done something for
Teddy that he could never forget.

Madeline's a

pies. Madeline

the grocer o

18 cents. What i

Madeline's a

pies. Madeline

the grocer

28 cents. What